THE HELEN KATE FURNESS
FREE LIBRARY
WALLINGFORD, PA 19086

W9-BPL-101

In honor of librarians

Sandi, Mary, + Lori

For the Kattam children of Lelboinet, my friends . . .
And for my own children, Sara, Corrie, Jake, and Luke, who once stayed in Lelboinet . . .—K.C.

For Joe, with love—J.D.

Text copyright © 2011 by Kelly Cunnane

Cover art and interior illustrations copyright © 2011 by Jude Daly

All rights reserved. Published in the United States by Schwartz & Wade Books,

an imprint of Random House Children's Books, a division of

Random House, Inc., New York.

Schwartz & Wade Books and the colophon are trademarks of Random House, Inc.

Visit us on the Web! www.randomhouse.com/kids

Educators and librarians, for a variety of teaching tools, visit us at

www.randomhouse.com/teachers

Library of Congress Cataloging-in-Publication Data

Cunnane, Kelly.

Chirchir is singing / Kelly Cunnane ; illustrated by Jude Daly. — 1st ed.

p.   cm.

Summary: Chirchir wants to help her family with their daily chores, but each

of their tasks proves too challenging for her.

ISBN 978-0-375-86198-7 (trade) — ISBN 978-0-375-96198-4 (glb)

[1. Family life—Kenya—Fiction. 2. Villages—Fiction. 3. Singing—Fiction.

4. Kenya—Fiction.] I. Daly, Jude, ill. II. Title.

PZ7.C91625Ch 2011

[E]—dc22

2009048989

The text of this book is set in Garamond Premier Pro.

The illustrations were rendered in acrylics.

MANUFACTURED IN CHINA

10 9 8 7 6 5 4 3 2 1

First Edition

CHIRCHIR IS SINGING

THE HELEN KATE FURNESS
FREE LIBRARY
WALLINGFORD, PA 19086

WRITTEN BY kelly cunnane ❧ ILLUSTRATED BY jude daly

schwartz & wade books · new york

High in Africa,
wind like a cat paw
wipes the sky clean.
Chirchir, Born Quickly, is singing,

Jambo! Hello! Day is growing tall.

Wake up to green sunlight and rooster's call!

"I'm going to help Mama today," Chirchir announces to Rooster,

whose feathers shimmer like fire.

And away she runs.

Warblers and cuckoos swing
    in the bottlebrush tree,
and Chirchir is singing.
Drop,
plop
the bucket in.
Wiggle it . . . jiggle it . . . Let it fill. . . .
Then hand over hand,
up comes
maji, maji—water!
She helps Mama lower the bucket
into the winking silver circle
of the well.

But—oh-ohh!

The rope slips,

water splashes,

Chirchir sprawls.

"Little one, this work is not for you," says Mama,

picking Chirchir up.

"Go help Kogo with the fire."

"I can do that," Chirchir says,

and away she scurries to her grandmother

as Crow calls out, "Caw, caw, caw! Ha, ha, ha!"

In the green leaves of the blue gum trees,

red-eyed and ring-necked doves coo,

"Koo-koo kooo! Koo-koo kooo!"

And Chirchir is singing.

My fire is hot!

Maize cobs snap and pop!

Boil water in a pot,

sprinkle leaves on the top.

Then make the chai

milky and sugary!

She helps Kogo build a fire

from twigs and old maize cobs.

But—oh-ohh!

The fire leaps too high,

chai sizzles and bubbles, then

shoosh,

boils over and—

Kogo's fire goes out.

"Littlest granddaughter, this work is not for you," says Kogo,

waving away the smoke.

"Go help Big Sister mud the floor."

"I can do that!" says Chirchir, and away she scuttles, cheeks hot,

as swallows on the roof call, "Tch, tch, tch! You spilled chai, chai, chai!"

In the blue-dark of the wattle trees,

yellow blossoms like little stars bloom,

and Chirchir is singing.

Hands go round and round,

smear the smoothest ground!

Flatten the deep red dirt

that smells of rain and earth!

She helps Ji-bet, Born in the Afternoon,

    spread a new floor

of cow dung and ashes in the kitchen hut.

But—oh-ohh!

"ACHOO!" Chirchir sneezes.

Mud flies into Chirchir's hair, up her nose,

onto her clothes, and . . .

all over Ji-bet too.

"Little Sister, this work is not for you," says Ji-bet,

wiping mud from her eyes.

"Go help Baba hoe potatoes."

"I *know* I can do that!" says Chirchir,

and away she hurries to her father,

face full of worry,

as monkeys laugh from above, "Ah, ah! Oo, oo!"

Wind whistles through cypress trees.

Maize leaves clatter like rain.

And Chirchir is singing

more quietly now.

Pale fat pumpkins, purple cabbage heads,

little green onions in seedling beds.

Sun shines on the garden rows.

Potatoes dug with a hoe!

She helps Baba by plopping potatoes into a sack for market.

But—oh-ohh!

Out roll the potatoes

one by one,

and off they go,

down the hill,

bumpity, bumpity.

"Littlest one," says Baba, frowning at the empty sack,

"just go play."

And he turns back to his work.

"I'm sorry," says Chirchir in a very small voice,

and away she slowly turns,

her smile upside down.

Under a scrap of tilted tin,

Hen lays a cream-colored egg.

Turkey ruffs his feathers into a big fan,

fiercely standing guard.

Everyone is working, even the animals.

And Chirchir is no longer singing.

Away she scuffs,

toes in the dust,

hanging her head

and swallowing her song.

But then

on the wind comes a sound,

sadder even than Chirchir.

What could it be?

Down from the garden,

over the fence,

across the little path,

and through the gate,

Chirchir runs,

toward the sound that grows

louder and sadder

until, inside the brothers' sleeping-hut,

she finds . . .

. . . Baby, Kip-rop, Born During Rain,
crying.
And there in the corner, fast asleep,
is naughty brother Kip-koech, Born at Dawn,
not watching Baby at all!

Gently, Chirchir picks up Kip-rop

and cradles him close.

And then once more, Chirchir is singing!

Everyone has work to do.

But I will sing my song for you.

Our house is nice and neat,

chai bubbles strong and sweet,

from the garden, lots to eat.

No worry, Baby, I will sing so you can sleep.

Chirchir's soft sweet sound soothes Little Brother.

"Cheka, cheka, cheka," he laughs like a little bird.

As Chirchir sings, her voice grows stronger,

mixing with the sounds of water splashing into buckets

and fires sizzling,

brooms sweeping dirt floors

and hoes digging potatoes,

swallows swooping,

families working,

and babies laughing.

At day's end,

when the clouds finally brush afternoon into evening,

Mama, Kogo, Ji-bet, and Baba all stop their work.

What has made the day pass so sweetly? they wonder.

The answer comes on a breeze

that echoes through the hills and valleys

of Kenya.

Chirchir is singing.

A NOTE ABOUT THE TEXT

Chirchir and her family are members of the Kalenjin tribe. Their buildings, their tools, and their chores are all typical of a present-day Kalenjin family living in the western highlands of the Great Rift Valley in Kenya.

Chirchir's family lives in a compound of small buildings, some of them used for sleeping and others for cooking. The kitchen floor is made from mud, ashes, and dung, an odorless and surprisingly resilient material once spread.

Hauling water from a well, washing dishes and clothes, gathering firewood, and tending young siblings while parents work in the field are all part of a child's daily life in rural Kenya. The competence and cheerful attitudes of my Kenyan friends have always impressed me; hence this story, to honor the daily work of the children of Kenya.

GLOSSARY

Members of the Kalenjin tribe speak their mother tongue, Kalenjin, and Swahili, Kenya's national language. The names here are Kalenjin, while the words used in conversation are Swahili. Kalenjin names reflect a defining aspect of a person's birth, such as the time of day or the weather. *Chi-* or *Ji-* often indicates a female name, and *Kip-* a male name.

Baba (BA-ba): Swahili for "Father."

Chai (rhymes with *eye*): A tea grown in the hills. It is brewed over a fire and served milky and sweet.

Cheka (CHEY-kaa): Taken from *kucheka,* the Swahili word meaning "to laugh." It is used here to represent Baby Kip-rop's laughter.

Chirchir (CHEER-cheer): Means "born quickly."

Jambo (JAHM-bo): Swahili for "hello." A common greeting in many East African countries.

Ji-bet (JEE-bet): Means "born in the afternoon."

Kip-koech (Kip-CO-aitch): Means "born at dawn."

Kip-rop (KIP-rop): Means "born during rain."

Kogo (KO-go): Kalenjin for "Grandmother."

Maji (MAH-jee): Swahili for "water."

12/11

E
CUN   Cunnane, Kelly
$24   Chirchir is singing

8/18

The Helen Kate Furness
Free Library
Wallingford, Pennsylvania   19086

GAYLORD

Delaware County Library System Media, PA

3 5918 11128 5997

5½
min.